The Sleeping Beauty

For my Mother and Father

First published 1993 by
WALTER McVITTY BOOKS
M/S 956, 41 Mill Hill Road, Montville, Qld 4560, Australia
Text and illustrations copyright © Margaret Early, 1993
Printed in Hong Kong by South China Printing Company Ltd

THE
SLEEPING
BEAUTY

&

Retold and illustrated

by

Margaret Early

WALTER McVITTY
BOOKS

NCE UPON A TIME there lived a King and Queen who were very unhappy — more than words can tell — because they had no children. They tried everything, seeking out doctors and healers all over the world; making vows to saints and going on pilgrimages to holy places, but to no avail.

At last, after many years, the Queen had a daughter, and a splendid christening was arranged. All the fairies who could be found in that country — just seven of them — were invited to be godmothers. As was the custom in those days, each would bring a special gift, and through these gifts the little Princess would be endowed with special qualities.

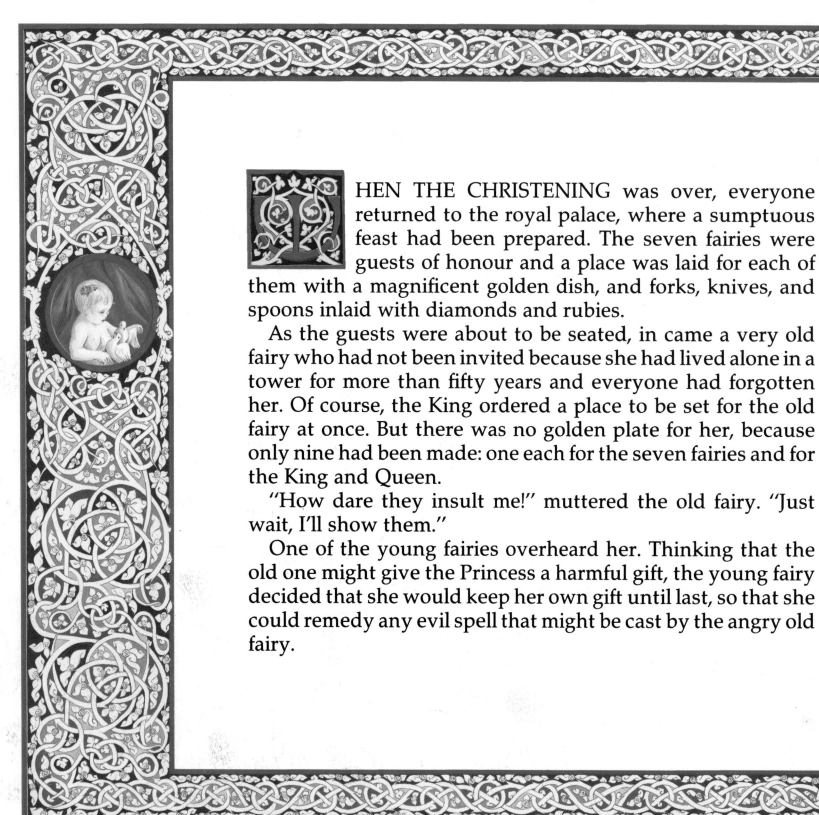

HEN THE CHRISTENING was over, everyone returned to the royal palace, where a sumptuous feast had been prepared. The seven fairies were guests of honour and a place was laid for each of them with a magnificent golden dish, and forks, knives, and spoons inlaid with diamonds and rubies.

As the guests were about to be seated, in came a very old fairy who had not been invited because she had lived alone in a tower for more than fifty years and everyone had forgotten her. Of course, the King ordered a place to be set for the old fairy at once. But there was no golden plate for her, because only nine had been made: one each for the seven fairies and for the King and Queen.

"How dare they insult me!" muttered the old fairy. "Just wait, I'll show them."

One of the young fairies overheard her. Thinking that the old one might give the Princess a harmful gift, the young fairy decided that she would keep her own gift until last, so that she could remedy any evil spell that might be cast by the angry old fairy.

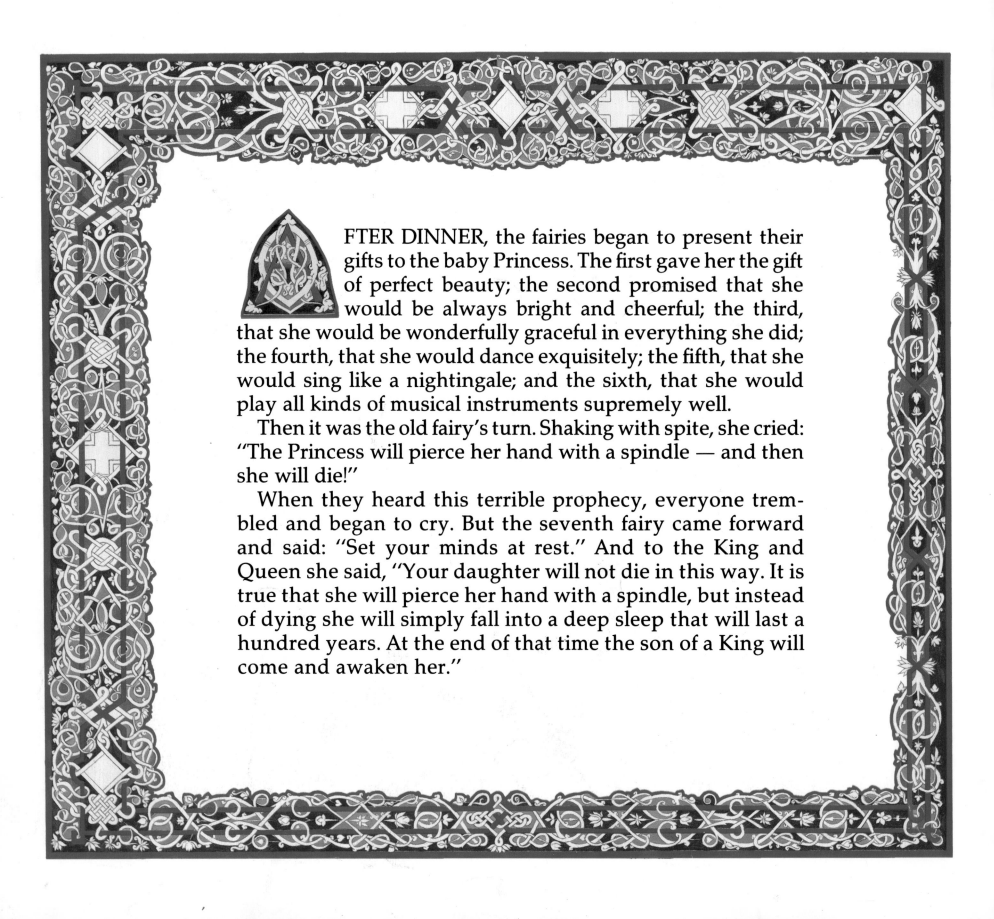

FTER DINNER, the fairies began to present their gifts to the baby Princess. The first gave her the gift of perfect beauty; the second promised that she would be always bright and cheerful; the third, that she would be wonderfully graceful in everything she did; the fourth, that she would dance exquisitely; the fifth, that she would sing like a nightingale; and the sixth, that she would play all kinds of musical instruments supremely well.

Then it was the old fairy's turn. Shaking with spite, she cried: "The Princess will pierce her hand with a spindle — and then she will die!"

When they heard this terrible prophecy, everyone trembled and began to cry. But the seventh fairy came forward and said: "Set your minds at rest." And to the King and Queen she said, "Your daughter will not die in this way. It is true that she will pierce her hand with a spindle, but instead of dying she will simply fall into a deep sleep that will last a hundred years. At the end of that time the son of a King will come and awaken her."

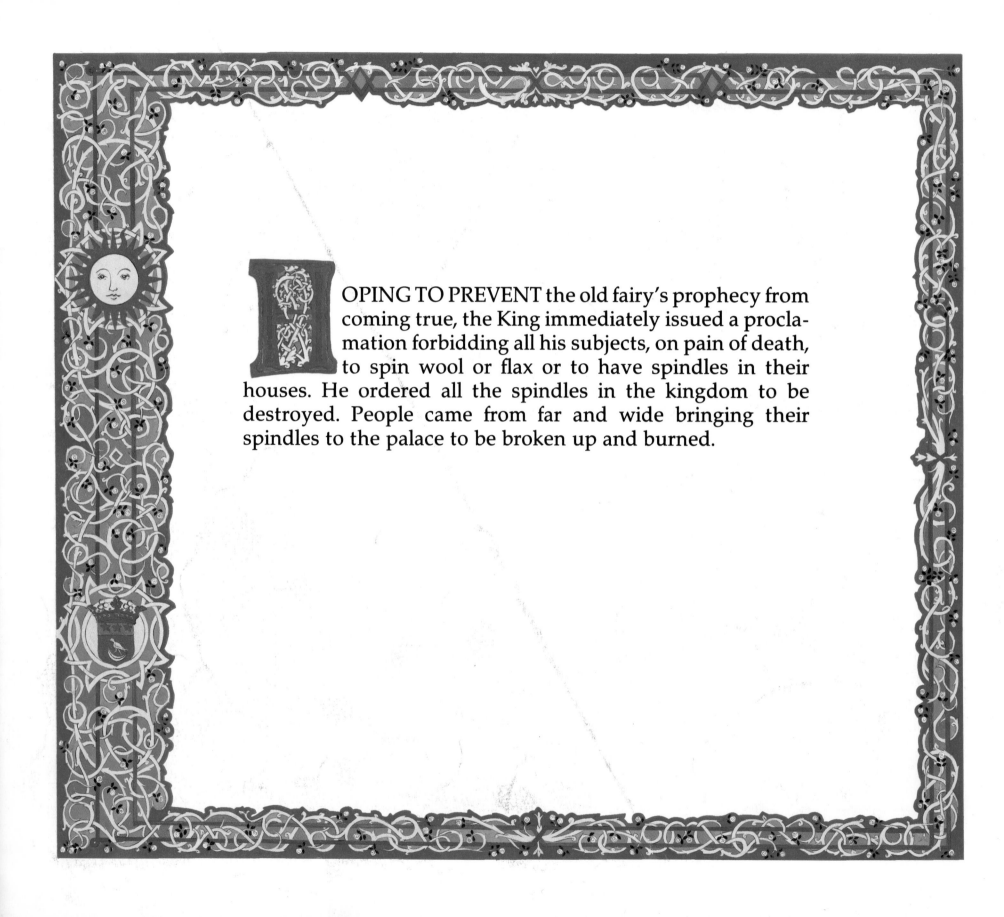

HOPING TO PREVENT the old fairy's prophecy from coming true, the King immediately issued a proclamation forbidding all his subjects, on pain of death, to spin wool or flax or to have spindles in their houses. He ordered all the spindles in the kingdom to be destroyed. People came from far and wide bringing their spindles to the palace to be broken up and burned.

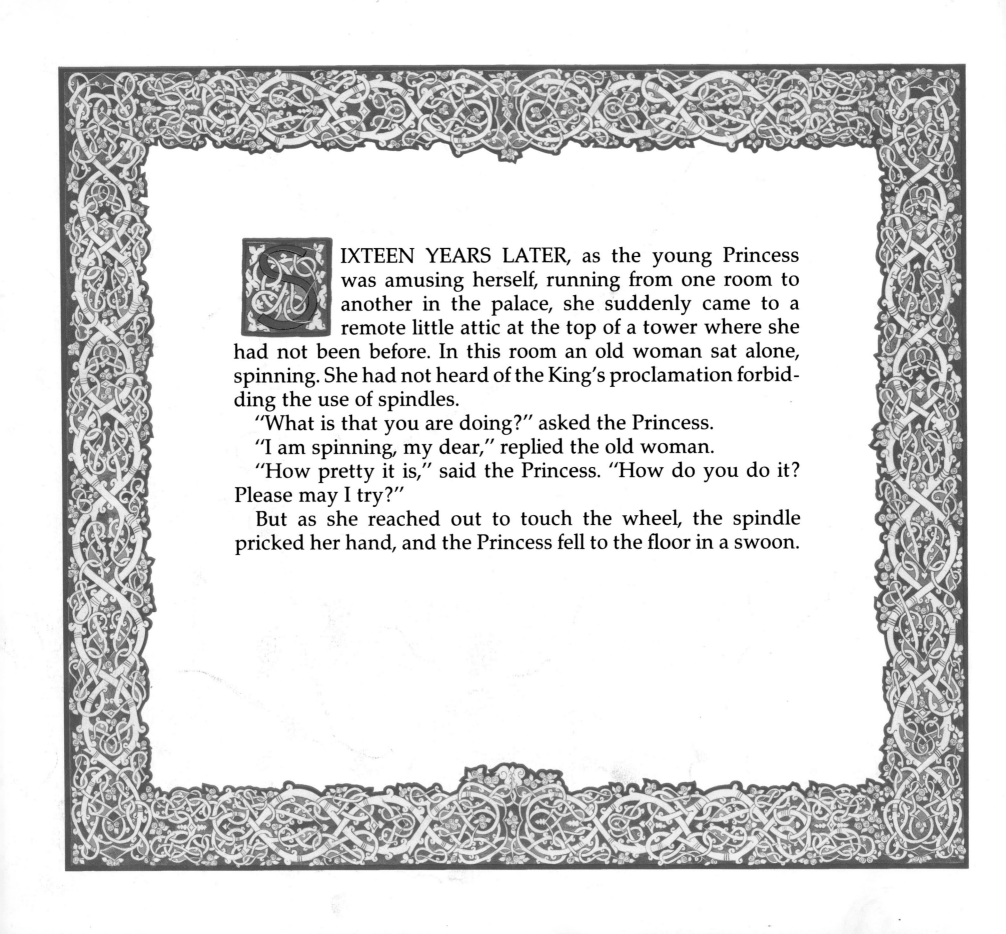

IXTEEN YEARS LATER, as the young Princess was amusing herself, running from one room to another in the palace, she suddenly came to a remote little attic at the top of a tower where she had not been before. In this room an old woman sat alone, spinning. She had not heard of the King's proclamation forbidding the use of spindles.

"What is that you are doing?" asked the Princess.

"I am spinning, my dear," replied the old woman.

"How pretty it is," said the Princess. "How do you do it? Please may I try?"

But as she reached out to touch the wheel, the spindle pricked her hand, and the Princess fell to the floor in a swoon.

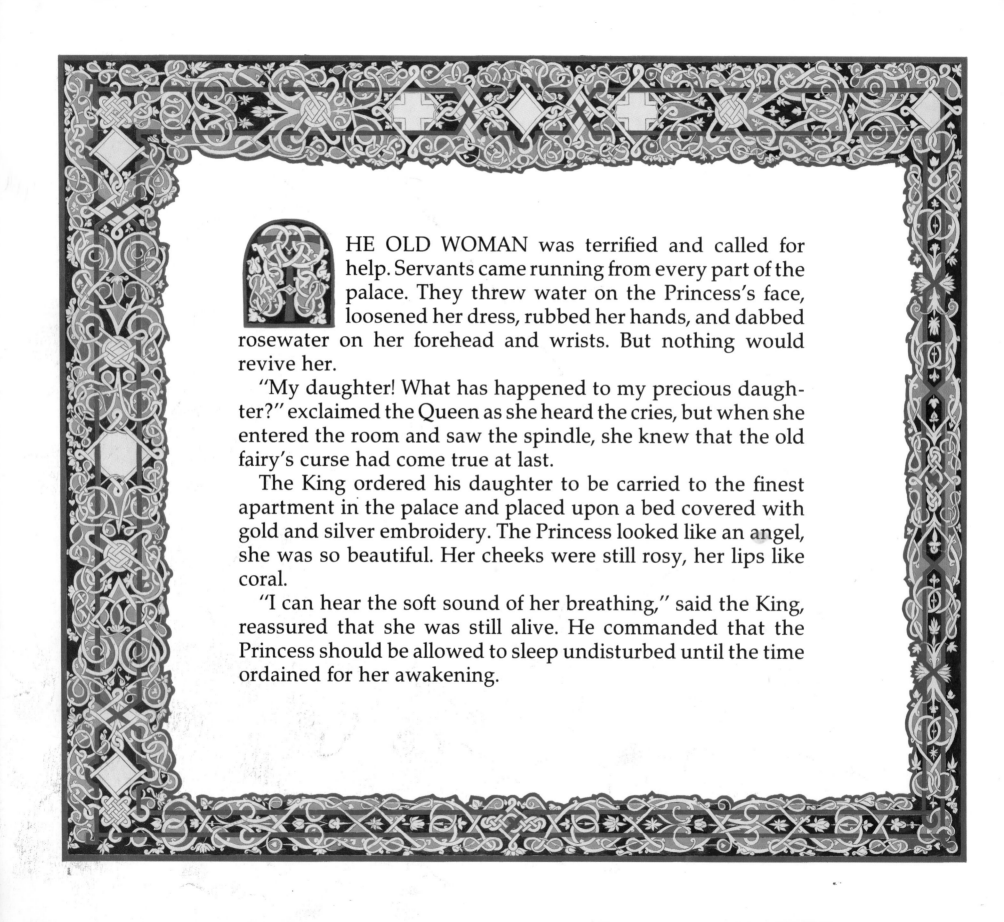

HE OLD WOMAN was terrified and called for help. Servants came running from every part of the palace. They threw water on the Princess's face, loosened her dress, rubbed her hands, and dabbed rosewater on her forehead and wrists. But nothing would revive her.

"My daughter! What has happened to my precious daughter?" exclaimed the Queen as she heard the cries, but when she entered the room and saw the spindle, she knew that the old fairy's curse had come true at last.

The King ordered his daughter to be carried to the finest apartment in the palace and placed upon a bed covered with gold and silver embroidery. The Princess looked like an angel, she was so beautiful. Her cheeks were still rosy, her lips like coral.

"I can hear the soft sound of her breathing," said the King, reassured that she was still alive. He commanded that the Princess should be allowed to sleep undisturbed until the time ordained for her awakening.

HE KING AND QUEEN then summoned the good fairy who had saved the Princess's life by giving her the gift of sleep for a hundred years.

"How sad the Princess will be if she awakens to find the castle empty," she said to them.

So, with her wand, she touched everything in the palace — the King and Queen, governesses, maids of honour, chambermaids, stewards, guards, doorkeepers, pages, and footmen. She touched all the horses in the stables, and the dogs as well — every living thing. The royal courtiers slept in the Grand Salon, and the musicians napped at their instruments. The cook let go of the mischievous kitchen boy and the scullery maid fell asleep as she plucked the feathers of a fowl. Food on the spit stopped cooking as the fire died down. All this was done in an instant, for fairy spells act quickly.

DENSE THICKET of trees and thorns and brambles grew around the castle, so tangled and twisted that neither man nor beast could enter. In this way the good fairy ensured that the Princess would have nothing to fear from the prying eyes of intruders while she slept.

A hundred years passed. Then, one day, a young Prince came hunting in a forest near the thicket. Over the trees he saw the palace's distant towers and inquired about them. Each person told him a different story, but most believed that beyond the entangled castle walls lived an ogre who ate children. The Prince did not know what to believe. Then an old peasant came forward and said:

"Your Highness, when I was a boy my father told me that in that castle there lies a most beautiful Princess, condemned to sleep for a hundred years until awakened by the son of a King."

HEN HE HEARD THIS, the young Prince felt certain that he was the very person destined to awaken the Princess. Determined to rescue her, he decided there and then to fight his way through the thicket. But as he lifted his sword to part the tangled thorns they drew apart as if by magic and let him through. The young Prince made his way toward the castle, which he could just make out at the end of a long row of trees. As he moved forward, the thicket closed in behind him, preventing others from following. He was all alone.

HAT THE PRINCE SAW when he reached the castle gate would have terrified the bravest person. Everything and everyone looked dead. The bodies of men and animals lay everywhere. But the Prince soon noticed that the guards and coachmen had red noses and ruddy cheeks. They were merely asleep. Listening carefully, he could tell that they were breathing. One of them could even be heard snoring softly.

 HE PRINCE THEN PASSED through a large court-yard, entered the castle's main door, and walked through one room after another. Wherever he went, he saw men and women fast asleep: some were on their feet, others were seated. In the kitchen he saw the cook still holding up her hand, about to scold the kitchen boy. He entered the Grand Salon, and saw the King and Queen, and the musicians and courtiers, all fast asleep. The only thing that broke the awesome silence was the gentle sound of their breathing.

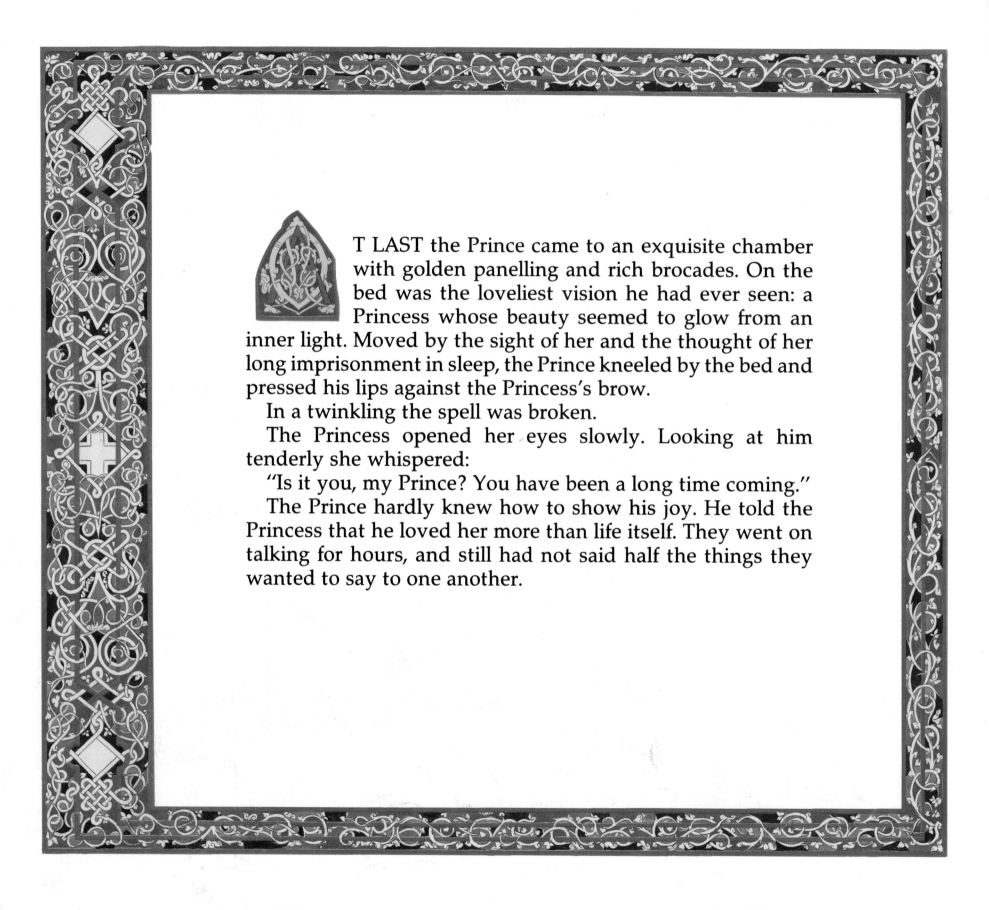

T LAST the Prince came to an exquisite chamber with golden panelling and rich brocades. On the bed was the loveliest vision he had ever seen: a Princess whose beauty seemed to glow from an inner light. Moved by the sight of her and the thought of her long imprisonment in sleep, the Prince kneeled by the bed and pressed his lips against the Princess's brow.

In a twinkling the spell was broken.

The Princess opened her eyes slowly. Looking at him tenderly she whispered:

"Is it you, my Prince? You have been a long time coming."

The Prince hardly knew how to show his joy. He told the Princess that he loved her more than life itself. They went on talking for hours, and still had not said half the things they wanted to say to one another.

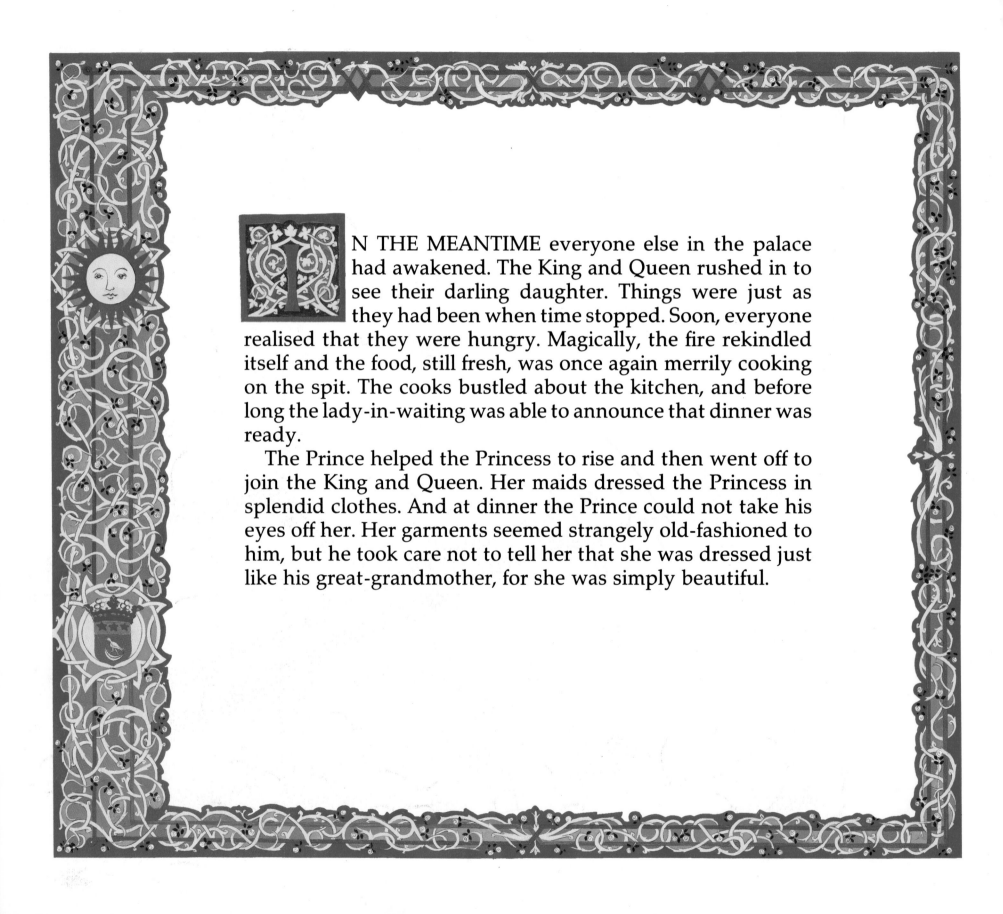

IN THE MEANTIME everyone else in the palace had awakened. The King and Queen rushed in to see their darling daughter. Things were just as they had been when time stopped. Soon, everyone realised that they were hungry. Magically, the fire rekindled itself and the food, still fresh, was once again merrily cooking on the spit. The cooks bustled about the kitchen, and before long the lady-in-waiting was able to announce that dinner was ready.

The Prince helped the Princess to rise and then went off to join the King and Queen. Her maids dressed the Princess in splendid clothes. And at dinner the Prince could not take his eyes off her. Her garments seemed strangely old-fashioned to him, but he took care not to tell her that she was dressed just like his great-grandmother, for she was simply beautiful.

S THE MUSICIANS played the old melodies that had not been heard for a hundred years, the Prince proposed to the Princess. At once the King summoned the palace chaplain and they were married without delay. For days thereafter the wedding was celebrated with great splendour and great joy. Since they had waited so long for their happiness, you may be sure that for the rest of their days they lived as happily as could be.

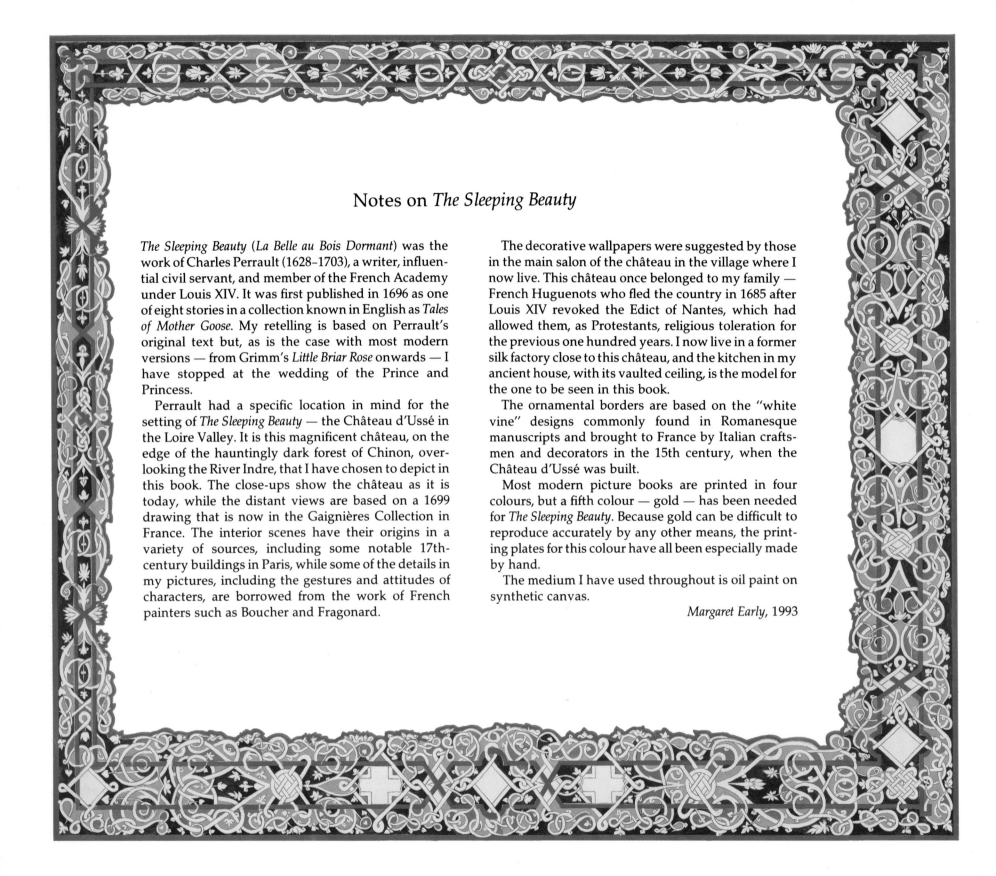

Notes on *The Sleeping Beauty*

The Sleeping Beauty (*La Belle au Bois Dormant*) was the work of Charles Perrault (1628–1703), a writer, influential civil servant, and member of the French Academy under Louis XIV. It was first published in 1696 as one of eight stories in a collection known in English as *Tales of Mother Goose*. My retelling is based on Perrault's original text but, as is the case with most modern versions — from Grimm's *Little Briar Rose* onwards — I have stopped at the wedding of the Prince and Princess.

Perrault had a specific location in mind for the setting of *The Sleeping Beauty* — the Château d'Ussé in the Loire Valley. It is this magnificent château, on the edge of the hauntingly dark forest of Chinon, overlooking the River Indre, that I have chosen to depict in this book. The close-ups show the château as it is today, while the distant views are based on a 1699 drawing that is now in the Gaignières Collection in France. The interior scenes have their origins in a variety of sources, including some notable 17th-century buildings in Paris, while some of the details in my pictures, including the gestures and attitudes of characters, are borrowed from the work of French painters such as Boucher and Fragonard.

The decorative wallpapers were suggested by those in the main salon of the château in the village where I now live. This château once belonged to my family — French Huguenots who fled the country in 1685 after Louis XIV revoked the Edict of Nantes, which had allowed them, as Protestants, religious toleration for the previous one hundred years. I now live in a former silk factory close to this château, and the kitchen in my ancient house, with its vaulted ceiling, is the model for the one to be seen in this book.

The ornamental borders are based on the "white vine" designs commonly found in Romanesque manuscripts and brought to France by Italian craftsmen and decorators in the 15th century, when the Château d'Ussé was built.

Most modern picture books are printed in four colours, but a fifth colour — gold — has been needed for *The Sleeping Beauty*. Because gold can be difficult to reproduce accurately by any other means, the printing plates for this colour have all been especially made by hand.

The medium I have used throughout is oil paint on synthetic canvas.

Margaret Early, 1993